...o are just starting on the amazing ...oks support both the acquisition of ...

The PURPLE LEVEL presents basic topics and objects using high frequency words and simple language patterns.

The RED LEVEL presents familiar topics using common words and repeating sentence patterns.

The BLUE LEVEL presents new ideas using a larger vocabulary and varied sentence structure.

The YELLOW LEVEL presents more challenging ideas, a broad vocabulary, and wide variety in sentence structure.

The GREEN LEVEL presents more complex ideas, an extended vocabulary range, and expanded language structures.

The ORANGE LEVEL presents a wide range of ideas and concepts using challenging vocabulary and complex language structures.

When sharing a book with your child, read in short stretches, pausing often to talk about the pictures. Have your child turn the pages and point to the pictures and familiar words. And be sure to reread favorite stories or parts of stories.

There is no right or wrong way to share books with children. Find time to read with your child, and pass on the legacy of literacy.

Adria F. Klein, Ph.D.
Professor Emeritus
California State University
San Bernardino, California

Editor: Jacqueline A. Wolfe
Page Production: Amy Bailey Muehlenhardt
Creative Director: Keith Griffin
Editorial Director: Carol Jones
Managing Editor: Catherine Neitge
The illustrations in this book were created with watercolor and colored pencil.

Picture Window Books
A Capstone Imprint
1710 Roe Crest Drive
North Mankato, MN 56003
www.capstonepub.com

All books published by Picture Window Books
are manufactured with paper containing at least
10 percent post-consumer waste.

Library of Congress Cataloging-in-Publication Data
Klein, Adria F.
Max goes to the library / by Adria F. Klein ; illustrated by Mernie Gallagher-Cole.
p. cm. — (Read-it! readers)
Summary: Max, who loves to read, discovers all the services available to him during
a visit to the library.
ISBN-13: 978-1-4048-1182-9 (library binding)
ISBN-10: 1-4048-1182-6 (library binding)
ISBN-13: 978-1-4048-3062-2 (paperback)
ISBN-10: 1-4048-3062-6 (paperback)
[1. Libraries—Fiction. 2. Books and reading—Fiction. 3. Hispanic
Americans—Fiction.] I. Gallagher-Cole, Mernie, ill. II. Title. III. Series.

PZ7.K678324Max 2005
[E]—dc22   2005003854

Printed in the United States of America in North Mankato, Minnesota.
072016   009875R

Max
Goes to the Library

by Adria F. Klein
illustrated by Mernie Gallagher-Cole

Special thanks to our advisers for their expertise:

Adria F. Klein, Ph.D.
Professor Emeritus, California State University
San Bernardino, California

Susan Kesselring, M.A.
Literacy Educator
Rosemount-Apple Valley-Eagan (Minnesota) School District

Picture Window Books
Minneapolis, Minnesota

Max likes to read books.

Max goes to the library.

He meets the librarian.

The name sign reads: Librarian

The librarian gives him a
library card.

The librarian shows him the children's books.

Max picks a book about animals.

He sits at the table and reads
his book.

Max uses a computer to find more animal books.

Max checks out three books.

Max wants to come back to the library very soon.

Max likes to read books.

WAIT!

DON'T CLOSE THE BOOK!

THERE'S MORE!

FIND MORE:

Games & Puzzles
Heroes & Villains
Authors & Illustrators

AT...

www.CAPSTONEKIDS.com

STILL WANT MORE?

Find cool websites and more books like this one at www.FACTHOUND.com
Just type in the BOOK ID: 1404811829 and you're ready to go!

7